The Adventures of Pennie

Clare Louise McAndrew
Illustrated by John Armin

First published in Great Britain in 2021
Copyright © Clare Louise McAndrew

The moral right of the authors has been asserted.
All rights reserved.

All characters and events in this publication, other than those clearly in the public domain, are fictitious and any resemblance to real persons, living or dead, is purely coincidental.
No part of this publication may be reproduced, stored in a retrieval system, or transmitted, in any form or by any means, without the prior permission in writing of the publisher, nor be otherwise circulated in any form of binding or cover other than that in which it is published and without a similar condition including this condition being imposed on the subsequent purchaser.

Editing, design, typesetting and publishing by UK Book Publishing
UK Book Publishing
www.ukbookpublishing.com
ISBN: 978-1-914195-47-1

The Adventures of Pennie

This is Pennie, a friendly Golden Labrador,

She is just as cute as can be!

She spends each day having amazing adventures,

Would you like to see?

Clare Louise McAndrew

She is a very clever dog and
can be mischievous at times.

Although she cannot talk to me in our language,
she is very good at acting out mimes!

You might have seen her on the village green or
near the park where she likes to play.

She is often seen roaming the beautiful
countryside along the trail called
'The Pennine Way'.

The Adventures of Pennie

She loves to go on long walks especially in
the heavy rain. Then when I'm not looking,
she stands next to me as she shakes
her wet smelly mane!

If you see her you may laugh and want to stare,
she really is such a hoot!

She splurges around in muddy puddles,
wearing her bright red Wellington boots.

She likes the game of fetching sticks,
the bigger the better in her smiley jaw.

Oh! and if you ask her nicely, she may give you
it and then offer you a filthy paw!

Clare Louise McAndrew

Her favourite sport is football;
she loves to watch it and play.

She likes to dart on to the pitch and pinch
the ball, then burst it and run away!

The boys and girls try to chase her,
she enjoys making them run.

You see her with her pink tongue hanging out,
panting and having so much fun!

The Adventures of Pennie

Sometimes when she feels bored,
she likes to play hide and seek in the house.

She climbs into the laundry basket,
curls up, trying to be as small as a mouse!

She likes to hear her name being called:
"Pennie, where are you hiding today?"

But it doesn't make her reveal herself,
she just giggles and decides to stay.

Clare Louise McAndrew

Pennie likes to teach road safety and help all the boys and girls cross the road.

She even helped the lollipop lady one day by scaring off an ugly green toad!

She gently went up to it and sniffed it with her wet chocolate-brown nose,

The toad was off as quick as can be scarpering on its creepy, long toes!

The Adventures of Pennie

Pennie's favourite place is at the beach,
she loves swimming in the cool, blue sea.

Then jumping out and drying off,
rolling around on the sand in front of me.

You better beware making model sandcastles
if Pennie is around.

She likes nothing better than flattening them,
creeping up when you are not looking,
not even making a sound!

Clare Louise McAndrew

Have you ever seen a dog on a skateboard?
Trying to balance and stay upright.

Then whizzing around, building up speed
and giving everyone a big fright!

Pennie likes to think she looks cool with her
stripy, bright sporty shoes.

She always has to wear four so she is lucky
that they are sold in twos!

The Adventures of Pennie

Pennie dreams of flying a brightly coloured
kite one day, with the ribbon tied to her collar.

Watching it glide through the air
making noises in the wind,
whispering its magic like holler!

She thinks about it floating up high,
feeling free and dancing in the open air.

It shimmers and shines and bounces around
like it doesn't have a care.

Clare Louise McAndrew

Pennie enjoys playing on the trampoline
and bouncing up and down.

She always makes everyone laugh,
acting like she is a clown!

She likes to jump as high as she can,
trying to grasp a loose branch from the tree.

Then falling with her bushy tail beneath her
legs and hoping no one can see.

The Adventures of Pennie

When the boys and girls are playing with their skipping rope, she dashes and tries to jump in.

Then all you see are arms, legs and furry paws flying, as she causes everyone to spin!

She watches as the children take a skip and a jump, one accidently let go of the rope.

She seizes the opportunity, grabs on to it and pulls, the children all tumbling, there really is no hope!

Clare Louise McAndrew

When the snow starts to fall Pennie gets
excited because she knows that can
only mean one thing...

Catching snowballs, building snowmen
and the best thing ever: going sledging!

She spins around and around,
chasing her tail with excitement,
as she plays in the soft fallen snow.

Eagerly awaiting her turn on the sleigh,
she keeps barking for yet another go!

The Adventures of Pennie

Pennie loves to have a bubble bath
and play with her bathtime toys.

A bright yellow duck and a squeaky fish
she was given by next door's boys.

She likes to jump in the paddling pool
and keep cool on a hot sunny day.

Splashing around and being naughty,
drenching everyone who gets in her way!

Clare Louise McAndrew

Then when the day is over and
Pennie feels sleepy and wants a cuddle.

She lies in her bed sometimes upside down
and puts all her blankets in a huddle.

She lies asleep in her comfortable bed
feeling warm, happy and secure.

You would never believe she could be such a
frolicsome dog; she looks so quiet and demure.

The Adventures of Pennie

Pennie dreams about all of her friends,
there are Mia, Whitney, Rosie and Sophie too.

Thinking about all the new adventures
they can have and what wonderful
things they could next do.

Her legs start to fidget and her eyes start to
twitch as she remembers the joys of the day.

She falls deeper asleep resting her tired furry
paws, ready for tomorrow's exciting play.

Coming soon!

The next instalment...

The Adventures of Pennie
- Farmyard Fun

Lightning Source UK Ltd.
Milton Keynes UK
UKHW020037021121
393202UK00007B/449